D0938568

I Dreamed I Was a Dog

"The universe is a dream dreamed by a single dreamer
where all the dream characters dream too."

–ARTHUR SCHOPENHAUER

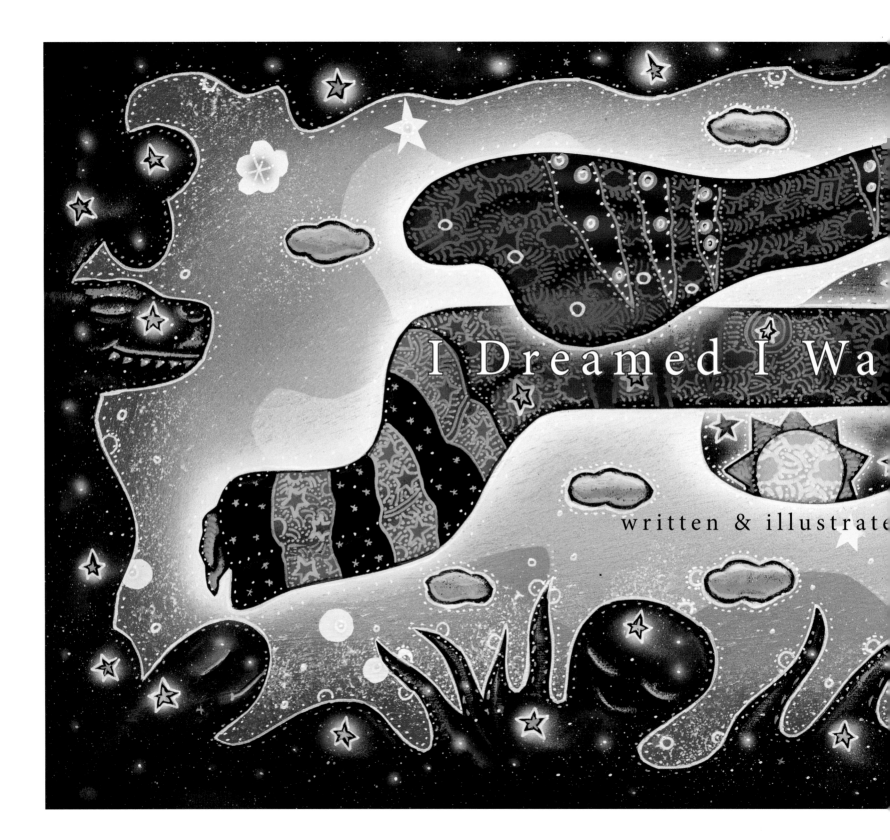

I Dreamed I Wa

written & illustrate

Dog

Joel Nakamura

LeafStorm
SANTA FE, NEW MEXICO

On a night of a million stars
and a million dreams . . .

I dreamed I was a dog.

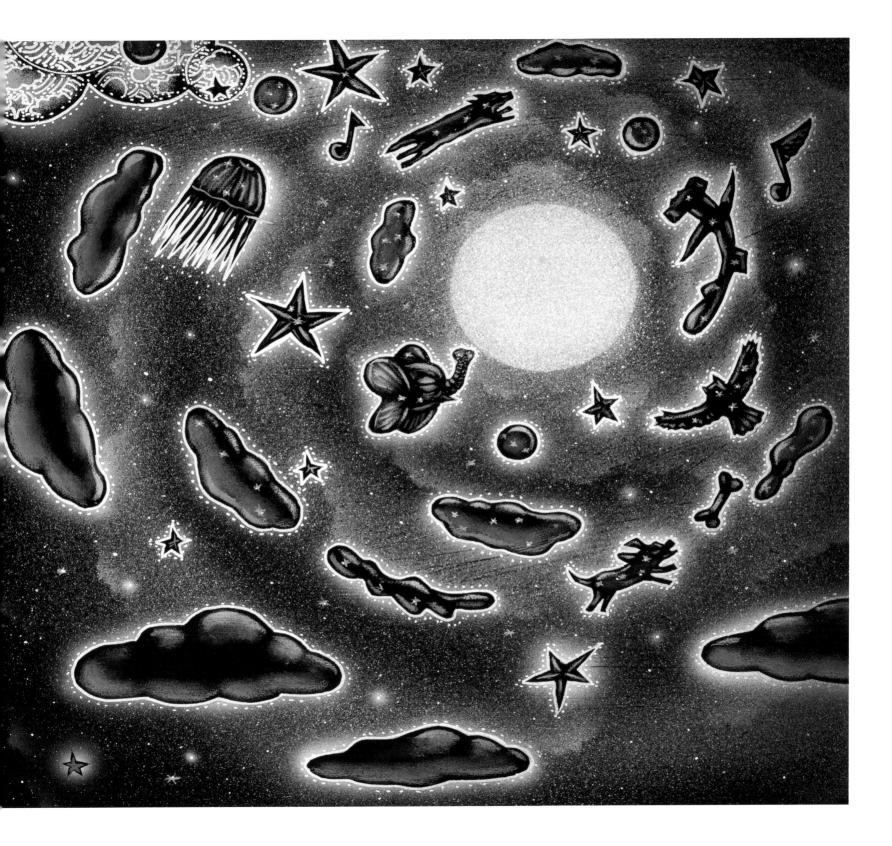

I dreamed I was a dog with red fur and purple spots, chewing on a giant bone.

Then suddenly I was a dinosaur
with a dog as my best friend.

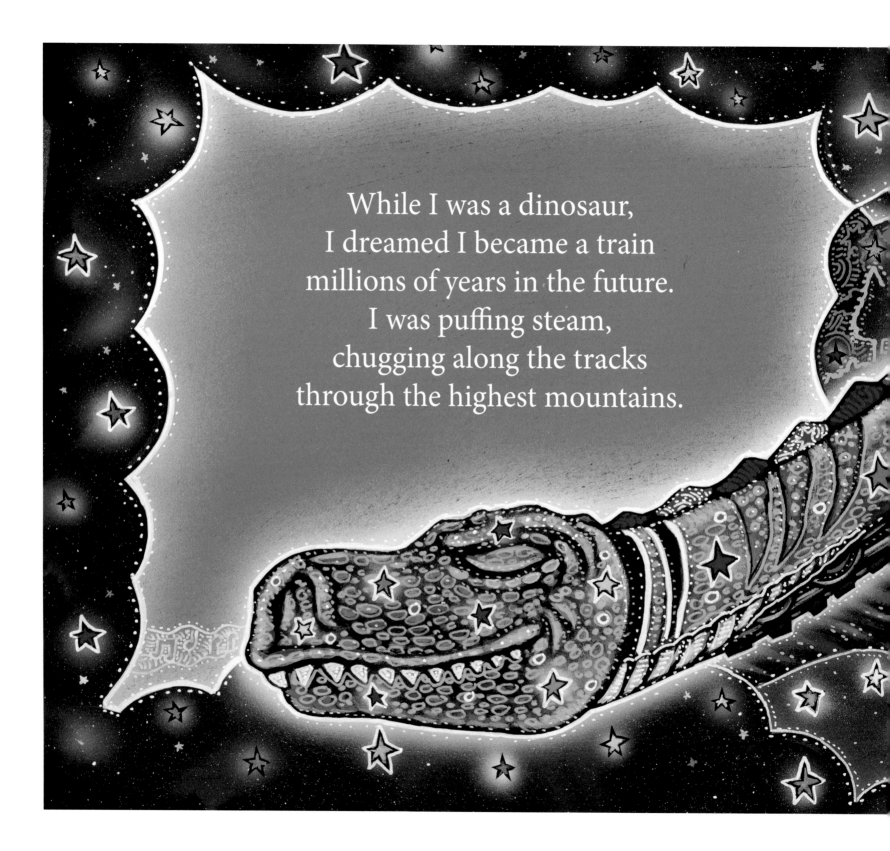

While I was a dinosaur,
I dreamed I became a train
millions of years in the future.
I was puffing steam,
chugging along the tracks
through the highest mountains.

While I was a train, I dreamed
I became a cloud.

I grew wings and flew high into outer space.

In space, I dreamed
I was a flying saucer,
spinning around a
purple planet.

While I was a flying saucer,
I dreamed I was a comet.
I sped through the cosmos with
a long sparkle of lights trailing
behind me. As I returned to Earth,
I dove deep down into the ocean.

And then I dreamed I was a whale,
singing songs under the sea.

I dreamed I was an ocean symphony.

Our music carried through the water and across the land into the savannah.

Then I dreamed I was an elephant,
remembering this dream.
I raised my trumpet and blew a stream
of butterflies across the grasslands.

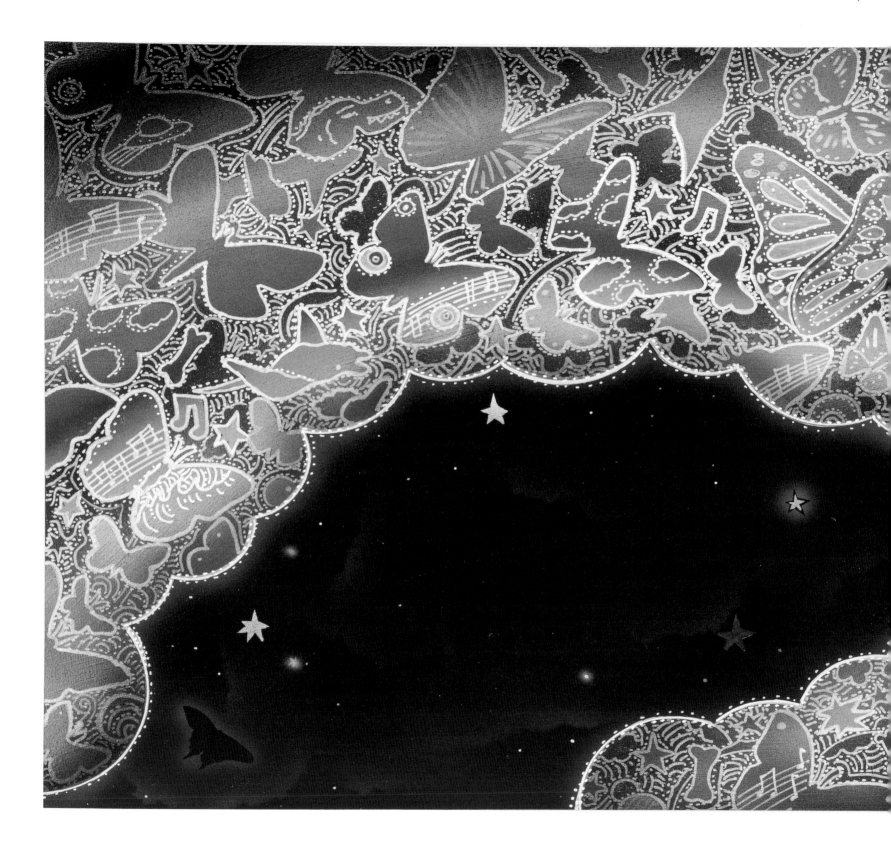

And then I dreamed
I was a bright butterfly,
landing on the head of a giraffe.

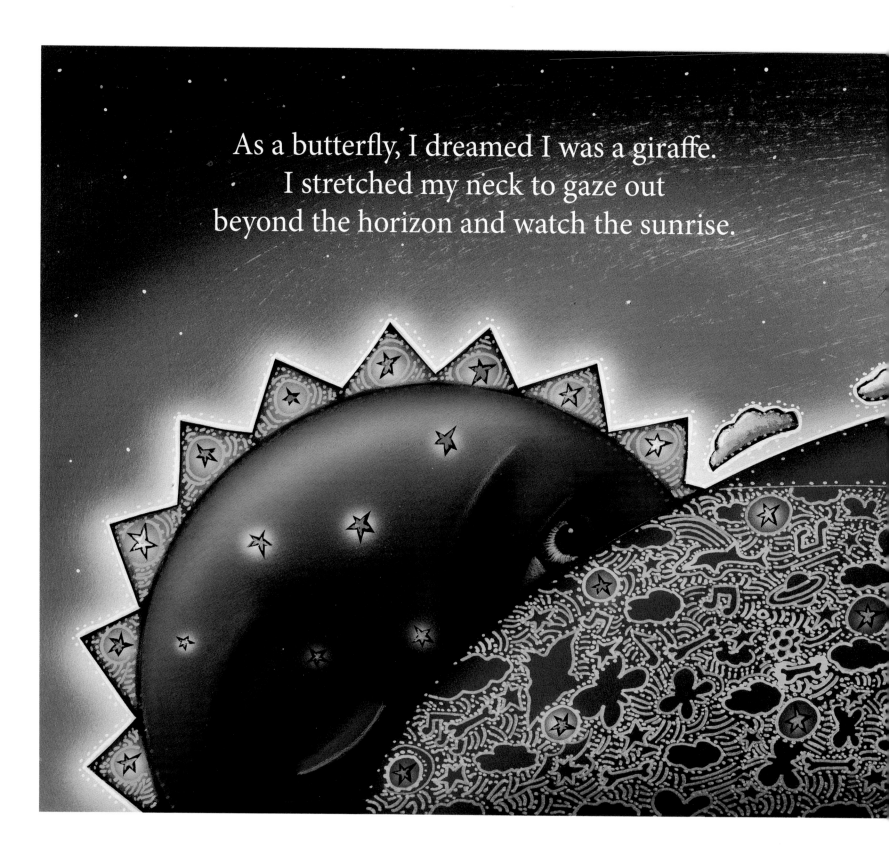

As a butterfly, I dreamed I was a giraffe.
I stretched my neck to gaze out
beyond the horizon and watch the sunrise.

Suddenly I was the sun, reaching gently through the window of a cozy house to wake up a red dog.

I opened my eyes.

The stars were gone, and the sun was shining brightly.

I was
myself
again,
here in
my room,
with my
special
friends.

In loving memory of my mom, Grace Nakamura, who always encouraged me to follow my dreams.

Copyright © 2017 by Joel Nakamura

Published by Leaf Storm Press
Post Office Box 4670
Santa Fe, New Mexico 87502
LeafStormPress.com

All rights reserved, including the right of reproduction in
whole or parts in any form.

Leaf Storm logo is a trademark of Leaf Storm Press LLC.

Leaf Storm Press books are available for special promotions and premiums.
For information, please email publisher@leafstormpress.com.

First Edition 2017
Book Design by LSP Graphics
Printed in Malaysia

10 9 8 7 6 5 4 3 2

Library of Congress Control Number: 2017946217
Publisher's Cataloging-in-Publication Data

Names: Nakamura, Joel.
Title: I dreamed I was a dog / Joel Nakamura.
Description: Santa Fe : Leaf Storm Press, 2017. | Summary: Joel Nakamura's vivid, colorful illustrations
transport readers on a magical journey that begins as a young boy falls asleep and dreams that he is a dog.
Identifiers: LCCN 2017946217 | ISBN 978-1-9456529-0-5 (hardcover)
Subjects: LCSH: Dogs--Juvenile fiction. | CYAC: Dogs--Fiction. | Animals--Fiction. | Dreams--Fiction. |
Nature--Fiction. | BISAC: JUVENILE FICTION / Animals / Dogs. | JUVENILE FICTION / Bedtime & Dreams. |
JUVENILE FICTION / Nature & the Natural World / Environment.
Classification: LCC PZ7.1.N35 Iab 2017 (print) | LCC PZ7.1.N35 (ebook) | DDC [Fic]--dc23.